JULIAN IS A MERMAID

Jessica Love

WALKER BOOKS
AND SUBSIDIARIES
LONDON • BOSTON • SYDNEY • AUCKLAND

This is a boy named Julian. And this is his Nana.
And those are some mermaids.

First published 2018 by Walker Books Ltd, 87 Vauxhall Walk, London SE11 5HJ • © 2018 Jessica Love • The right of Jessica Love to be identified as the author and illustrator of this work has been asserted by her in accordance with the Copyright, Designs and Patents Act 1988 • This book has been typeset in Godlike • Printed in Italy • All rights reserved. No part of this book may be reproduced, transmitted or stored in an information retrieval system in any form or by any means, graphic, electronic or mechanical, including photocopying, taping and recording, without prior written permission from the publisher. • British Library Cataloguing in Publication Data: a catalogue record for this book is available from the British Library • ISBN 978-1-4063-8063-7 • www.walker.co.uk • 10 9 8 7 6 5 4

Julian LOVES mermaids.

"Let's go, honey. This is our stop."

"Nana, did you see the mermaids?"

"I saw them, honey."

"Nana, I am also a mermaid."

"I'm going to take a bath. You be good."

Julian has an idea.

"Oh!"

"Come here, honey."

"For me, Nana?"

"For you, Julian."

"Where are we going?"

"You'll see," says Nana.

"*Mermaids,*" whispers Julian.

"Like you, honey. Let's join them."

And they do.